BIG MONTY AND THE MALICIOUS MUSIC TEACHER

Copyright © 2022 by Homestead Books

All rights reserved.
This book or any portion thereof may not be reproduced
or used in any manner whatsoever without the express
written permission of the publisher, except for
the use of brief quotations in a book review.

Printed in the United States of America

First Printing, 2022

ISBN: 978-1-7350983-4-0

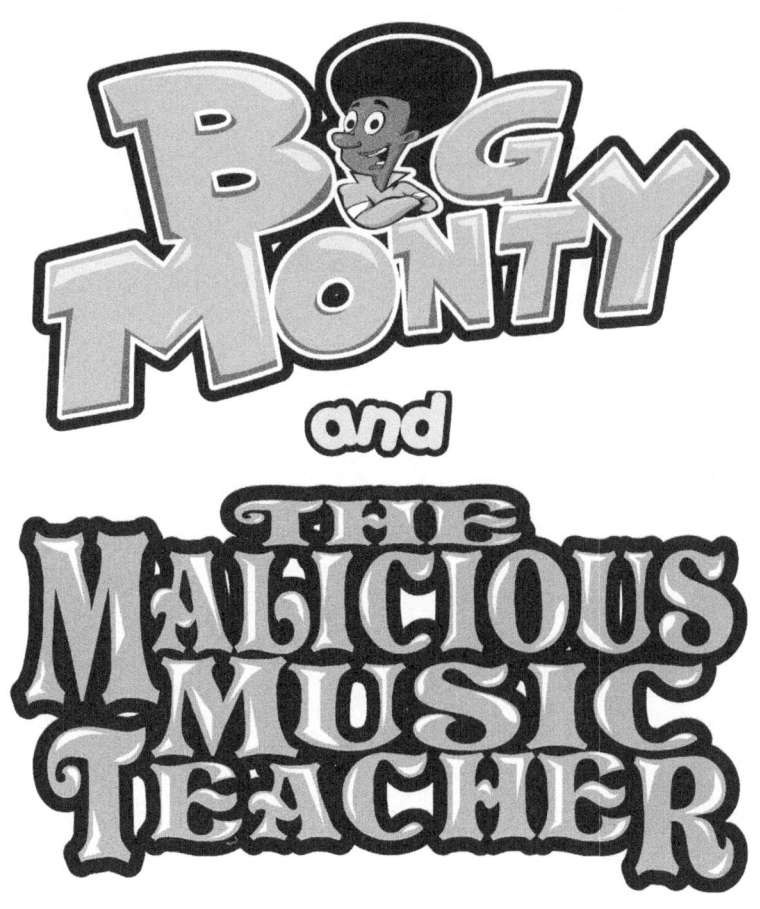

BIG MONTY and THE MALICIOUS MUSIC TEACHER

BY
MATT MAXX

TABLE OF CONTENTS

1. Mad for Music and an Upcoming Competition — 1
2. Playing Second to a Little Sister with Big Talent — 9
3. A Fool in Love and Two Doses of Trouble — 17
4. Something Suspicious and One Familiar Feeling — 23
5. Trance Music and Hot Wings — 29
6. Piecing Together One Weird Puzzle — 35
7. A New Attitude for One Wired Diva — 43
8. Spoken Word and A Choir of Angels — 51
9. Merlin Steps Out and Josephine Takes Over — 59
10. Two Detectives and One Mad Merlin — 69
11. Where Merlin Loses it and Roly Comes Undone — 75
12. A Mortified Merlin and One Radical Rapper — 87
13. No Good Plans for One Hypnotized Class — 95
14. Last Ditch Efforts and All Tapped Out — 103
15. Real Wins and True Lessons Learned — 111

CHAPTER 1

Mad for Music and an Upcoming Competition

I was making my way down the south wing of Washington Carver Elementary School to the music room when Mabel knocked me flat and beat me to the door. That girl spends more days suspended than in school. Still, she loves music class along with every other false pretender (AKA wannabe) in my school.

I peeled myself off the floor and opened the music room door. My best bro, Global, sat in the front row with his crazy-tail self, playing his funky bassoon. FYI, a bassoon is a musical instrument in the woodwind family. Never heard of it? Me neither. It figures that Global chose the most random instrument to play. I went to put my backpack down under my chair, and that's when I heard her. Roly Hayes, the newest girl in 5th grade, was practicing scales with our music teacher, Ms. Dottie.

Word is that Roly transferred to our school just to be in the choir conducted by Ms. Dottie. Apparently, Ms. Dottie was related to some big-time jazz singer named

Ella Fitzgerald. No cap! I had no idea who Ella Fitzgerald was until my mom played some songs for me on Spotify. Ella was a real deal jazz singer in the 1930s and was called "The Queen of Jazz."

Before I get too carried away, my name is Merlin Montgomery, but I go by Big Monty for you new folks. If you missed out on why I go by my nickname instead of my government name, go back and check out the other Big Monty Books. But, seriously, would you go by Merlin if your parents did that mess to you?

Unlike my classmates, science is more my thing. But, music is what's hot at Washington Carver Elementary School. We live in the best music city on the planet, Memphis, TN. Music class is no joke at my school. We take music seriously—especially competitions. Check out the end of this chapter to find out more about some famous Memphis musicians.

Last December, smack dab in the middle of the winter concert, our old music teacher,

Mr. Marley, started doing some weird stuff during the choir's music set. This dude placed the little white baton in between his toes and conducted the chorus with his feet! I know. Just nasty. FYI, the music baton is that wand-looking stick that choir directors wave in front of the musicians.

We weren't actually too surprised since most of us had already heard about the lunchroom incident the week before. Instead of monitoring kids' behavior during lunch, Mr. Marley stood in a corner talking to the trash can about buying the new album that he and his ham sandwich produced. For some reason, the principal still let him work the winter concert where Mr. Marley really put the "cuckoo" in cuckoo clock. Long story short, we had a new music teacher when we came back from winter vacation.

Our new music teacher, Ms. Dottie, is one of those teachers that can inspire a skunk to take a bath. We all loved her! Even Mabel behaved in her class. Word is that Miss Dottie is Washington Carver Elementary's best shot at winning the city-wide music competition.

But, I had bigger things on my mind. Roly Hayes. I had to figure out a way to get her to talk to me. I'm not the best singer in the choir, but I am not the worst by far. The award for the worst singer in our grade definitely goes to A'Lo. In music class, you can always find A'Lo's short self in the middle of the room singing at the top of his lungs with those broken earpods hanging on for dear life on the sides of his crooked head. I am still baffled that none of his friends think he is weird. Baffled is another word for being confused.

I ignored the sound of A'Lo's cry for help, I mean singing, and sat down beside Global and his funky bassoon. "Hey, Big Monty," Global said out of breath. Clearly, that bassoon takes a lot of energy out of him. But, at least it's not as bad as Jordy Jones, who plays the tuba. Once, back in October, Jordy overate candy at Halloween. I guess it upset his stomach because when he blew into that tuba, he let one! Man, he will never live that down.

"'Sup, Global?" I asked, watching Roly review music at our teacher's desk.

"I see you are checking out our new classmate, Big Monty," Global nudged me in the ribs, then burst out laughing. "She is very accomplished. I think she takes private lessons." He can read me like a book since we've been best friends for like, ever.

"What are you laughing at?" I looked away from Roly's perfect teeth and ponytail.

"Dude, you got it bad for Roly," Global said. I pretended like I didn't hear him while Ms. Dottie rapped her baton on the music stand to get the class to settle down before warm-ups.

Memphis is known as the birthplace of rock 'n' roll, but the city has influenced music worldwide. Elvis Presley, Al Green, Isaac Hayes, Bruno Mars, and Moneybagg Yo have all created music here in Memphis. Do yourself a favor. Google Memphis music icons and take a listen. Let me know who you discover, and I'll tell you my favorite over on the FB or IG pages for Matt Maxx Books.

CHAPTER 2

Playing Second to a Little Sister with Big Talent

Ms. Dottie tapped her music stand again. We all stood, stretched, and warmed up to Ms. Dottie's favorite song, "Lean On Me," by some guy named Bill Withers. The song is old school, but it's grown on me. You would guess that no one would be into stretching and singing in unison with the characters in my class like A'Lo and Mabel. It's goofy, like one of those 90's boy bands my mom listens to while she cleans.

But, even Mabel gets really into it. Let's be honest; she has as much rhythm as Carlton on the Fresh Prince. Of course, that doesn't stop her slinky self from waving her arms from side to side like she's at a concert. It is so weird because this is literally the only class Mabel participates in.

I'm not a horrible singer, but being next to Roly made me nervous. She sat in the front row, right in front of Global and me. Instead of singing out like everyone else, I just lip-synced. Lip-synching is when you pretend to sing by moving your lips without actually making a sound. Mabel's stretches got a little out of control, and she knocked Ms. Dottie's Bluetooth speaker over. I didn't notice the music had stopped at first because I was so distracted by Roly. I just kept moving my big mouth with enthusiasm until I realized Ms. Dottie was staring right at me.

After music class, everyone slated for lunch, but Ms. Dottie asked to speak with me at her desk. Great. I was letting the best teacher in my school down. My parents would give it to me for lack of effort in school when they heard about this.

"Big Monty, may I speak with you for a moment about the competition?" Ms. Dottie asked, waving me to her desk covered in music sheets and competition trophies. Ms. Dottie is the only teacher in the entire school that calls me Big Monty. It made me feel even worse for disappointing her.

Ms. Dottie stood a foot taller than me and wore oversized hoop earrings and red lipstick that made her teeth look very white. As I got closer, I noticed her canine teeth were a little longer than expected. Canine teeth are the pointed ones next to your front teeth. For a split second, it reminded me a little of a vampire in one of my comic books.

"Yes, Ms. Dottie?"

I'd never gotten in trouble in class before this year. Still, I was beginning to get a reputation because of the whacky behavior of the adults in my school. Getting in trouble was more Mabel and A'Lo's thing.

I did not want to be sent to Principal Williams' office one more time this year. When you get sent to the office, they make you sit in the hallway on this raggedy old bench while they call your parents. Every student in the school passes that bench. A'Lo is the king of walking by that bench to check students. I could hear A'Lo now, "AYE MeRliN! I knew your singing was bad, but DANG, they're gonna suspend you for attempted ear assault. HAHAHAHA!"

I approached her desk as she lifted an envelope and handed it to me. *OH NO!* I panicked. A letter to my parents! The writing on the front of the tan-colored envelope read "To the Parents of Josephine Montgomery." Phew!

"Big Monty, I need you to give this letter to your parents. It is a permission form. It's to allow your sister to recite her award-winning poem, "Memphis Bred, Memphis Fed," as a spoken word piece backed by music at the competition." She flashed her canines at me in a big smile.

I was so relieved I wasn't going to have to hear my dad fuss. "Sure, Ms. Dottie. I'll give it to Josephine as soon as I see her."

I shoved the envelope in my backpack and ran out the door to catch Global at lunch. "Thank you, Big Monty," Ms. Dottie called out. "I knew I could count on you." I smiled big at the thought of even being noticed by Ms. Dottie and waved goodbye.

My little sister is Josephine Montgomery, the genius. Josephine is not your typical 2nd grader and not your average annoying little sister. Being the older brother to a genius may seem cool, but having a little sister who reads on a higher grade level than you and enjoys the same subject as you but does it better can be rough. Let's not forget how she is always trying to hold my hand in public, which is far from fabulous. I try my best not to encounter her during the school day, but it's becoming more and more difficult these days ever since she wrote that poem for the mayor's reelection last year. That poem of hers earned her an award AND a little fame on social media. Now don't get me wrong, I love my little sister. But if I have to hear that poem one more time . . .
I'm more of a science guy. So here's a cool experiment you can try at home

Cloud in a Bottle

Here's what you'll need to see it for yourself:

- Empty plastic water bottle with cap
- Scissors
- Isopropyl rubbing alcohol
- Safety goggles

Instructions:

1. Remove the label from the plastic water bottle.
2. Put on your safety goggles or safety eyewear.
3. Pour a small amount of alcohol into the bottle.
4. Put the cap on the bottle.
5. Slowly rotate the bottle, so the alcohol coats the inside of the bottle.
6. Grab the bottom one-third of the bottle and twist. This will create pressure in the bottle.
7. Release and watch your Cloud-in-a-Bottle form right before your eyes.

CHAPTER 3

A Fool in Love and Two Doses of Trouble

I hurried down the hall with my Neil deGrasse Tyson backpack. Most people don't even realize that my pack is themed because it's just black with a little image of the galaxy on each shoulder strap, which is why I picked it. It screams science nerd, but I don't care. Nerds like

Neil deGrasse make bank, and that's what I plan to do.

Neil deGrasse Tyson is an astrophysicist, meaning he studies the universe like the stars and the planets. Some people will say that he is responsible for the planet Pluto losing its planetary status.

Do y'all remember learning about planets in 2nd grade? "My very educated mother just served us noodles." That sentence helped us remember the eight planets were **M**ercury, **V**enus, **E**arth, **M**ars, **J**upiter, **S**aturn, **U**ranus, **N**eptune. Well, guess what? There used to be nine. My mom told me it used to be "My very educated mother just served us nine pies." Pies was for Pluto, but it got demoted. Personally, I like pies better then noodles, and I like Pluto as a planet! I guess we take out the pies and change the nine to NOTHING. "My very educated mother just served us nothing!" Sorry, I am a little upset about Pluto's demotion. Word is they made it a planet again, but who knows what they may change next.

Anyhoo. Avoiding trouble for my fake singing in class made me happy, but I still felt down about music class. Everyone in our class seemed to have some talent. Even tone-deaf A'Lo had so much confidence that it made up for his lack of skill. Now, to kick a brother while he was down, even my sister was included in the competition. I needed to do something to impress Ms. Dottie other than just being the brother of the genius girl.

I was deep in thought on my way to the cafeteria, so I almost jumped out of my skin when I heard, "Big Merlin?" I froze and nearly swallowed my tongue. It was Roly! I just stared at her like some kind of armadillo caught in headlights. "Hi, Big Merlin. Is that right?"

"Uh... um, it's Merlin. I MEAN BIG MONTY," I blurted out, trying to correct myself before my gawd-awful name got stuck in her head.

She giggled, "Oh, my bad. I wasn't really sure." I couldn't believe I was finally talking to her! "I wanted to ask you a question about the competition. Would you be interested in practicing with me sometime in music class? I don't have a lot of friends in the class yet, but you seem to get along with everyone," Roly said.

I couldn't believe it. Roly thought I got along with everyone. Did that mean she thought I was popular? Not wanting to miss my chance, I yelled, "You got it, Roly!" Ugh, I sounded like such an idiot!

She laughed again but didn't seem to be weirded out by how lame I was acting. "Sounds great, Big Monty."

I was watching her walk away when I felt a yank on my backpack that landed me on my tail. I looked up from the floor to see A'Lo and Mabel leering at me. A'Lo had the envelope for my parents in his hand. "Hey BIG MERLIN!" he mimicked Roly, "You left your nerdy backpack open."

"Bruh, that ain't funny. Give that back, A'Lo!" I said, scrambling to my feet. Talking to Roly had given me a bit of confidence, and I didn't feel like taking A'Lo's smack today.

"What is this anyway? A permission slip? You don't need this. You sound like a chicken crowing in music class anyway!" A'Lo joked as he ripped up the permission slip, letting the pieces fall to the floor. Mabel was beside him pretending to be a chicken, yelling,

"COCK A DOODLE DOOOO!" They both laughed and walked like chickens through the cafeteria doors.

CHAPTER 4

Something Suspicious and One Familiar Feeling

Man, that A'Lo can really be a piece of work. He doesn't even know that chickens don't crow. "Roosters crow, not chickens, you doof!" I called after the doors swung closed. I never can think of comebacks at the moment. That ever happen to you?

I picked up the pieces of what was left of the permission slip and booked it like A.J. Brown at the NFL Combine to the music room, which I regretted later due to scuffing my brand-new Air Force Ones. But, I wasn't about to let Ms. Dottie down.

Strange music played when I walked through Ms. Dottie's closed classroom door. All the lights were off, but I could see Ms. Dottie hunched over her keyboard in the back of the room by the window playing some eerie notes. The tune sounded slightly like our competition choral set but with random sounds in between. Ms. Dottie kept repeating those same odd notes throughout our music set.

"Ms. Dottie?" I called as I walked slowly through the music room door. Immediately, Ms. Dottie stopped playing. She brushed the music sheets off the keyboard onto her lap faster than Mabel hiding answers to a test written on her arm before the teacher came around.

"Merlin!" she stammered, "What are you doing here?" This was one of the few times I had ever seen Ms. Dottie's face without a smile. It was also the first time she had called me Merlin since she called roll on her first day in class.

"I had a bit of a situation," I said, showing her what was left of the permission slip. "May I have another permission slip for Josephine?"

Ms. Dottie hurried to her desk, rummaged through papers, and handed me a new form. "Thanks," I said.

Right before I walked out the door, Ms. Dottie called out in a stern, quiet voice, "Also, Merlin, be sure to knock next time." Shocked by her tone, I nodded my head in acknowledgment and closed the door. The back of my neck prickled. I got an all-too-familiar feeling that something wasn't right once again at Washington Carver Elementary. There was only one person I knew who could help me figure out what was going on.

SOMETHING SUSPICIOUS AND ONE FAMILIAR FEELING

When Ms. Dottie played that strange music, the feeling I got reminded me of the same feeling I got earlier this year. When I heard our lunch lady, Mrs. Findlehorner, speaking to her food monster hologram that she created to take out all the kids who complained about school lunch in Big Monty and the Lunatic Lunch Lady. That reminded me of this cool science experiment:

3D Hologram Projector

Here's what you'll need:

- Adult Supervision is very important for this experiment!
- Plexiglass CD Case
- A smartphone

- Scissors
- Tape or super glue

Instructions:

1. Cut the CD case into 4 triangles.
2. Cut the tip off of the top of each triangle so that the very top is flat.
3. Glue or tape the sides of each triangle together to create a pyramid with no point at the top.
4. Open a fun video on your phone of lightning or a cartoon character.
5. Lay your phone flat with the video on pause.
6. Place the flat top end of your pyramid projector in the middle of your phone.
7. Press play on the video displayed on your phone and enjoy your projection.

CHAPTER 5

Trance Music and Hot Wings

The line for Josephine's Polka-dot Paraphernalia (AKA gear) was more than 20 kids deep, which was really saying something on hot wings day. Josephine sold her signature polka-dot bows, headbands, socks, and anything else she could put polka-dots on to raise money for our school nutrition program. In other words, she helped our lunch lady increase the budget for school lunch. That meant we didn't eat the nasty stuff every other school served. Lunch at Washington Carver was prime.

I watched Josephine take payment for a yellow and purple polka-dot bow. Then, I pulled her over to the lunch table where Global sat, with wing sauce all over his face. Josephine cut her eyes at me just like our mom does when I forget to let the dog out. "Merlin, what the what are you doing interrupting prime sales time?" she said, holding a wad of cash in her hand.

I didn't waste any time. "Guys, I have a bad feeling something trippy is about to go down at Washington Carver again."

"Impossible!" Global said, struggling to swallow the mountain-sized bite in his jowls (AKA huge cheeks). "The odds that another supernatural, or scientifically unexplainable event could happen at our school in my estimation are about one in a hundred-thirty-eight-thousand."

"Listen. Just now, I went to the music room to get a letter for Josephine about the choir competition. I saw Ms. Dottie doing some crazy-people-stuff on the keyboard."

Josephine perked up. "Really? What is the letter for? Let me see it!"

Josephine wasn't listening. "That's not what's important right now! I think Ms. Dottie was doing some mind-tricking stuff with the keyboard. What do they call it?" I pondered, then I yelled out, "A trance! Trance music."

Josephine dug the letter addressed to her and our parents out of my backpack, "Merlin, what you are saying doesn't make sense. Ms. Dottie is a level-headed educator who recognizes true talent. Why else would she ask *me* to perform spoken word at the competition?"

I pulled out my phone and googled, "Listen up! A trance can be described as a state of hypnotism and blurred consciousness. It can be triggered by spiritual meditation, psychedelic drugs, some breathing techniques, or even occur almost randomly. Trance music mimics this state by building up tension through a series of build-up beats and release layers."

"A trance?" Global shook his head. "Ms. Dottie is one of the most normal, nicest, and best teachers around. There is no way she would be playing around with trances."

"YO! NO CAP!" A'Lo's fake gold tooth blinded me as he stuck his short neck into my conversation. "Just because you sing like a dying parrot doesn't mean that Ms. Dottie is some crazed competitor like Coach Hamhock who would stoop to mind-tricks."

At this point, I didn't know what else to say. "Dude, I know what I heard. She was playing these weird notes in between our music set." I pleaded with my classmates, trying to get them to believe me.

"That actually makes sense, bruh," A'Lo said. "There is no way we can win when the judges hear your busted-up voice during our set. She probably has to hypnotize them into thinking you can actually sing." Mabel, sitting beside him with a hot wing in each fist, started to choke from laughing.

"Whatever, A'Lo," I said, "I know what I heard." I thought A'Lo and I might be cool by now with all our adventures saving Washington Carver Elementary together. Still, every time I think A'Lo has come around, he acts completely whack.

CHAPTER 6

Piecing Together One Weird Puzzle

I slumped down into a lunch table bench, grabbed a wing off of Global's plate, and started chewing. I couldn't believe no one believed me after all the deep-space stuff we had seen at this school: lunatic lunch ladies, pumped-up principals, and a cyborg substitute. How did I become the one who looked crazy?

Global said, "Did you hear it might snow this weekend?" It never snows in Memphis. I guessed my friends were too excited about the possibility of sledding down hills on sheets of cardboard to care about another teacher-turned-villain.

"Great," I said. "We might get snowed-in at school with a malicious music teacher."

Josephine took pity on me. She grabbed my hand and said, "Merlin, let's go to Ms. Dottie's room and check out what you think you saw." Wiggling my hand out of hers, I followed Josephine out the cafeteria, leaving Global to his wings and A'Lo and Mabel to their hyena laughter.

Ms. Dottie's door was already open this time. I followed my sister, but the hair on my arms stood up, and I felt a shiver. "Josephine!" Ms. Dottie beamed, "I am so glad you are here. Did you get the permission form?"

Josephine responded in her annoying professional voice, "Yes ma'am, I certainly did. Thank you so much for allowing me to perform. I made Merlin escort me right down here to thank you in person."

Ms. Dottie looked me up and down. "Big Monty, I would expect you to be eating lunch after running up and down the hallway all morning," she said. But hearing her call me "Big Monty" no longer felt right.

"Yes ma'am. I was able to get a bite or two in."

Ms. Dottie eased over to her keyboard and slowly sat down. She said, "The lunch bell will be ringing soon. You all should get to your next class, and I have another class coming in soon." Josephine happily waved goodbye to Ms. Dottie and trotted out the door.

Maybe I was off. Maybe all the strange things at school this year were making me paranoid. I turned to glance back at Ms. Dottie once more. She lifted both hands, smiled at me with her long teeth, and struck a loud, eerie chord on the keyboard. An electric shock, like a lightning bolt shot through my entire body.

All of a sudden, I felt ... powerful! Then, in a voice like Daniel Caesar, I belted out in perfect tune, "See you later!"

Ms. Dottie cheesed up like she'd just won the pick-six. "See you later, Merlin."

PIECING TOGETHER ONE WEIRD PUZZLE

Speaking of snow. Here's a cool experiment where you can make your own.

LET IT SNOWSTORM IN A BOTTLE

Here's what you'll need:

- Clear Plastic bottle with straight sides
- White washable paint
- Water
- Popsicle stick
- Disposable cup
- Baby oil
- Alka-seltzer tablet
- Adult supervision

Instructions:

1. Pour some white washable paint into the cup.
2. Add some water to the cup to thin the paint.
3. Use the popsicle stick to mix the paint and water.
4. Pour the paint into the clear plastic bottle until the bottle is about 1/4 full.
5. Tilt the bottle and gently add baby oil until the bottle is about 90% full. Try not to mix the baby oil with the paint.
6. Drop one half an Alka-Seltzer tablet into the bottle and enjoy.
7. Repeat as many times as you like.

CHAPTER 7

A New Attitude for One Wired Diva

"Morning, Big Monty! I can't believe you beat me here," said Roly as she entered the room, placing her backpack decorated with tiny music notes on the ground. We had agreed to meet a few minutes before music class to warm up when I DMed her last night.

"You know I show up to get it done like Ja Morant against Golden State," I said, dribbling an imaginary basketball and taking a jump shot.

"Wow! I didn't realize you were so into the competition. Nice! Well, let's get started. I'll play some keys on the keyboard, and you can match the note," Roly said as she sat at the keyboard in the back of the room.

She played a C note on the keyboard. I filled up my chest with air and belted out a pitch-perfect C. Roly looked up at me in shock, "WOW, Big Monty! That was amazing!"

"Well, you didn't think that with looks like mine, I would be a bad singer like A'Lo, did you?" I raised one eyebrow at her like I'd been practicing in the mirror for months. Roly frowned a bit but kept going.

"Honestly, I didn't know what to expect. I've never heard you sing before." We continued running though our musical scales until class began, and I nailed every note Roly threw at me like whack-a-mole.

The bell rang, and the class raced into the music room. Global went straight to his bassoon and started tuning it up. Roly gathered her music sheets and moved to her seat. I followed behind her and sat next to her. I looked back at Global and gave him a thumbs up.

"Yo, Merlin! You think if you stand next to Roly, no one will be able to hear how bad you sing?" A'Lo snarked as he slunk into the room. Half the class started to laugh, but the laughter stopped almost immediately as Ms. Dottie took her place in the front of the class.

"Naw Bruh, I'm just saving her from your bad breath." The other half of the class roared.

Ms. Dottie winked at me. Then, she began discussing our music set for the competition. "Today, we will skip warm-ups to reserve time to rehearse our competition set. Thank you to Roly and Big Monty for coming in early today to warm up in preparation for our competition," said Ms. Dottie.

"TEACHER'S PET!" A'Lo yelled, pretending to cough.

I stood and turned to the class.

> *"Don't hate because my talents deserve recognition.*
> *Just fess up that yours are worth demolition!"*

The class laughed, and I took a bow. It looked like one of A'Lo's busted-up earbuds finally decided to kick the bucket. You could see the wiring hanging out as he stuffed them into his ears and slumped into his seat.

I scooted my chair even closer to Roly after that beatdown, but she moved hers away. "You seem kind of different today, Big Monty."

Global leaned over his bassoon and put his giant head between us, "He has become what is officially called a prima donna in the musical world. Prima donnas are more commonly known as divas or someone who thinks they are all that and a bag of chips."

"Diva? What is your beef?" I glared at Global. "Keep blowing your horn, little boy."

Ms. Dottie started the music for the first set on her Bluetooth speaker. The first song featured the girls in the class that sang alto

and soprano. Next, came a part for boys who sang the low baritone parts. I was naturally a tenor meaning that my singing voice was slightly higher.

At the end of the first set, Josephine walked into the classroom dressed fresh to def. Josephine had on her brand-new pink and white Jordans with matching polka dot knee socks. Mom had pressed her khaki school shorts that she matched with a pink and purple collared shirt with her business's name on the front pocket. Finally, she set it all off with two purple and white polka-dotted bows in her hair braided into two large afro puffs. You would have thought today was the actual competition.

"Josephine, you may have a seat at my desk until it is your turn to perform," Ms. Dottie told her.

The next song was my time to shine. Again, the tenors took the lead during this song while most girls sang alto, meaning their voices were softer to help create the right melody.

Ms. Dottie started the music, and I let my voice rip. By the second verse, everyone fell quiet but me. A'Lo pulled one earpod out to see what the commotion was about, and his mouth dropped open wide enough to fit his entire fist into it. Ms. Dottie smiled from ear to ear, watching Big Monty blow the class away. The song ended, and the class broke out into applause.

"Big Monty! That was amazing! You sound better than Bruno Mars," Global said in shock. Everyone except for A'Lo seemed to be impressed. He turned up his beats and checked out.

I saw Josephine slip out of her seat. She motioned to me that she was going to check her hair in the bathroom. Obviously, neither A'Lo nor Josephine could handle being totally outdone by my talent.

CHAPTER 8

Spoken Word and A Choir of Angels

After my first-class performance, I knew I had Roly's attention. So I flipped my collar up and gave her my coolest smile, "Roly, there must be something wrong with my eyes, 'cause I can't take them off you." Roly looked thoroughly confused, so I tried again,

"Do you know what my shirt is made of? It's made of boyfriend material."

Roly looked like she ate something bad. Global dragged his bassoon past me and said, "Cool it, Big Monty. You're making an absolute imbecile of yourself." What did he know? He'd been wearing the same brown, too-short pants since the second grade, and he only found some cool points a few months back when he defeated our pumped-up principal.

"Alright, class, our next song is a musical set with the piano and Global on the bassoon." Global took his place at the front of the class next to Ms. Dottie at the keyboard. Ms. Dottie waved her director's wand with one arm and began to play. The first notes she hit sent an electric shock through the entire class. Everyone jolted upright, and the entire class sang out in unison, "LAAAAAA," in *perfect* harmony. Next, global began playing his bassoon like he was a part of BB King's Blues Band.

As Global finished his solo, Josephine slipped back into the class right at the end of the set. "Josephine, it is your turn to perform," Ms. Dottie said. She placed the class podium and mic stand in the center of the room, and Josephine took her place.

Josephine's Spoken Word

> "Memphis bred, Memphis fed
> We live in the birthplace of rock 'n' roll.
> I have been told
> From young and old,
> That rock 'n' roll feeds the soul,
> Much like a hot, buttered roll.
> Jackie Brenston sounded great,
> He made people croon with "Rocket 88"

And Sister Rosetta Tharpe,
She added her heart.
Music is the food of the soul,
It's the perfect remedy for sadness for
those young and old.
If you are listening to anything I say,
Please know Memphis loves music in
every way,
So drop a beat and go cray-cray!"

The class applauded at the end of Josephine's soliloquy. A soliloquy is when a person expresses their thoughts aloud by themselves as if no one else is in the room.

Ms. Dottie moved the microphone stand and took her place back in front of the class to begin the music for our final song. The song started slowly but picked up with the high and melodious voices of the sopranos taking control. Mabel belted out like Beyonce while Roly harmonized with her like Jazmine Sullivan. Everyone started staring at A'Lo, who was singing entirely out of tune. He registered the attention, slid an earbud out, and realized he was the only one off key. A'Lo started lip-synching.

In complete shock, Josephine said, "WOW! You guys sound like Chloe x Halle, but even better." A'Lo's beady eyes darted in disbelief back and forth between Ms. Dottie, me, Josephine, and the rest of the class.

Ms. Dottie beamed as the class held the last note for almost 30 seconds. Finally, the song ended, and she thanked the class for a fantastic rehearsal right before the bell rang for lunch. As soon as the class was dismissed, Josephine hurried over to me. "Merlin, what in the world was that? The choir sounded like the gospel choir singing behind JeKalyn Carr."

"What are you talking about? We sound like we always sound," I said. "Maybe you've just never appreciated my Grammy-award-winning voice. Ms. Dottie is the first teacher with the highly skilled ability to properly train a choir."

"Grammy-award-winning?" Josephine's eyes were huge. "Who are you? And what have you done with my brother?"

"Whatevs, little sister. You just can't handle being outshone for once in your life." I grabbed my bag and hurried toward the door to score a seat next to Roly at lunch, but Josephine cornered me.

"Merlin!" She looked like a light bulb went off above her afro puffs. "I think this is exactly what you were saying yesterday! Ms. Dottie must have put you and the class in a trance so you could sing better!"

"I have no idea what you are talking about," I said. Jamal Jenkins would beat me to a seat if I didn't hurry, but A'Lo came up and blocked the door.

"Bruh, what kind of soul-singing steroids are you and the rest of the class taking?" A'Lo glared at me.

"I don't know what you guys are talking about, but one thing is for sure, A'Lo. You've got some major work to do if you want to be a part of the competition choir. You're as tone-deaf as a dying donkey, and it's not about to ruin our chance at winning the choral competition. So you better step up or stay home." Brushing past A'Lo's shoulder, I walked out the door to lunch.

Not everyone can sing like me. But if you want an easy way to improve your sound, check out this website on Top Apps to Make Your Voice Sound Better, by Joey Sturgis.

https://joeysturgistones.com/blogs/learn/top-apps-to-make-your-voice-sound-better

CHAPTER 9

Merlin Steps Out and Josephine Takes Over

"**Did he just tell me to step MY game** up? Also, I know he did NOT bump my shoulder," yelled A'Lo angrily.

"A'Lo, see? Something is definitely wrong here," Josephine wrinkled her forehead, thinking hard.

"BET! The old Merlin wouldn't dare talk to A'Lo like that."

Hold up, guys. It's me, Josephine, here. If you haven't noticed, we are in a bit of a predicament. A predicament is a tough situation. Merlin has completely lost his marbles. My big brother has never shown this much bravado before in his life. He has gone from Mr. Science-Nerd to acting like our classmates are begging for his autograph. Until we can figure out what to do about Merlin and Ms. Dottie, I'm going to take over the story.

I grabbed A'Lo by the arm and pulled him into the hallway. A'Lo mumbled, "Man watch it! This is a brand-new fit."

"A'Lo, something is definitely wrong here. We have to figure out how to fix it," I said.

Straightening out his shirt that was clearly two sizes too small, he interrupted, "Fix it? Naw, girl. I'm about to be famous. Did you hear Mabel? I bet I can record them and get some kind of artist finding fee or something."

"A'Lo snap out of it!" I yelled. "This is serious! If they are really in some kind of hypnotic trance, then our school can get in trouble for cheating. If we get caught cheating, that means everyone is in trouble!"

"What do you mean, everyone? I didn't do this," A'Lo crossed his arms over his too-small shirt.

"It doesn't matter who did what! We are part of that class, and we will all be in trouble. With your record, you may have to repeat the 5th grade," I told him.

Choking on his spit, A'Lo yelled out, "AHH NAW FAM! I ain't getting held back! Bruh, what do we need to do to fix these folks?"

We hurried down the hall and caught up to Merlin before he made it to the cafeteria. "Merlin, Miss Dottie says you need to go to the library because the school newspaper wants to interview you for tomorrow's front page." I lied.

"Naturally! Can't keep my public waiting," Merlin said. A'Lo rolled his eyes. I thought that little tough guy was going to blow a gasket if he had to listen to any more of Merlin's self-hype.

The library doors were much larger since the school remodeled the entire library after the principal went crazy a few months ago. "Bruh, this is nice!" A'Lo said as I pushed through the library doors.

"Have you seriously not been in the library in three months?" Like I should have been surprised. I walked to the check-out desk where our school librarian mumbled to herself. Since the incident with Principal Williams, Mrs. Anthony had developed a weird tic where the slightest noise would cause her to scrunch her shoulders up to her ears and hold them there.

"Mrs. Anthony," I said politely. Her shoulders shot to her ears. "May we use the computers for a project?"

She turned around, "Oh Josephine, it's you!" Her shoulders relaxed. "So nice to see you. Of course, you and your little classmates here can use the computers."

A'Lo and I took a seat at the computer furthest from anyone in the library. "Who was she calling little?" A'Lo asked.

"And where's my interviewer?" asked Merlin, pacing behind us. "Don't people know my schedule is very tight?"

I tried to ignore Merlin and logged into the computer. A search for "Ms. Dottie" and "choir director" brought up nothing. "That must not be her real name," I sat stumped.

"Of course not," A'Lo snorted. He whipped out his broken-down wallet and pulled out a driver's license featuring a picture of Ms. Dottie and the name Milena Davis.

"A'Lo, how did you get that?" I was scared. A'Lo's tactics were ruining my chance at an Ivy League scholarship by the nano-second.

"Don't freak out. It's expired. I finessed it out from behind Ms. Dottie's current one. She'll never miss it. I am NOT re-doing the 5th grade over this uber-competitive music maniac."

I typed "Milena Davis, Choir Director" into the search bar of the web browser. As we waited for the results, Merlin started getting really agitated. "What kind of sorry, unprofessional . . . late to an important . . ."

"Merlin, calm down, dude," A'Lo said.

"Calm down? I'll finish him! Pain does not exist in this dojo!" Merlin yelled. Miss Grenrich's shoulders shot up to the ceiling, and she hurried toward us, shushing Merlin.

"What the?" A'Lo shook his head in disbelief. "He thinks he's in some kind of musical Cobra Kai!"

"You guys, look! I found Ms. Dottie." A'Lo slid his chair closer to the computer while Mrs. Anthony tried to calm down Merlin's enormous ego.

The search pulled up an article that read, "American Idol Favorite Milena Dorothea Davis Breaks Family Legacy."

A'Lo turned to me. "Translate for me, Big Brains."

Josephine Here. Since I'm telling this chapter, I'm putting in my added activity at the end. My big brains aren't limited to schoolwork. I can focus them on all sorts of important things, like fashion! Here's a recipe for making an old t-shirt into something fabulous using tie-dye. You're welcome!
From https://www.thesprucecrafts.com/how-to-tie-dye-1245650

Tye-Dye

Equipment / Tools

- Apron/old clothes that you don't mind accidentally getting dye on
- Rubber gloves
- Large pot or bucket (one per dye color)
- and/or squeeze bottles

Materials

- Item to dye that's at least 60% cotton
- Dye enhancer, such as soda ash or sodium carbonate (optional)
- Fabric dye (in one or more colors of your choice)
- Rubber bands or string
- Plastic bag/plastic wrap

Prepare the Dye

1. Prepare your dye as directed by the manufacturer. You can either mix dye directly in a large pot or bucket or mix it in a plastic squeeze bottle for more targeted dye application. The instructions on your dye will typically state which method is best.

2. Tie Your Item

3. Now it's time to twist and tie your item. You can choose to tie parts of the fabric in an irregular manner or aim to form a specific pattern.

4. For instance, to make a spiral pattern with the dye, lay out your fabric completely flat and find its center. Then, using a fork or your fingers, grab the center and swirl it until the fabric is rolled in a circular shape. Use your rubber bands or string to secure the fabric in this shape. The ties should meet in the middle of the fabric, forming an asterisk.

Start Dyeing

Now your item is ready for the dye. Either dip it in your dye container or apply the dye from the squeeze bottle. Fully cover fabric in dye. If you are using multiple colors, it's usually best to start with the lightest one. Check your manufacturer instructions for how to proceed to the next color; you might have to rinse the fabric or pause for a period of drying time.

CHAPTER 10

Two Detectives and One Mad Merlin

I scanned the article, searching for more context. "It looks like Ms. Dottie is related to the famous musician Miles Davis on her Dad's side. She comes from a line of famous singers and songwriters on her mom's side, including Ella Fitzgerald. This woman has musical genius in her veins!"

"But what does it mean when it says 'breaks family legacy' she didn't win?" asked A'Lo.

"Not exactly. It looks like right before the season finale, it was discovered that all of the contestants except for Ms. Dottie experienced nervous breakdowns," I summarized.

"It says here that Ms. Dottie's greatest competitor would randomly start clucking like a chicken during the season finale rehearsals. Also, the other finalist pretended to play a saxophone instead of singing their final set."

"SWEEP THE LEGS," Merlin yelled. And Ms. Anthony ran with her shoulder stuck in lift-off out of the library.

"BRUH! STOP!" A'Lo called back to him. "Wait. Do you think Ms. Dottie did the hippopotamus thing with those singers just to win?" A'Lo asked.

"It is called hypnosis, and I am starting to believe she did. I bet she figured out some way to sneak subliminal hypnosis into her musical chords."

"Speak English, Homegirl."

"I am most certainly not your homegirl. Subliminal means below the threshold of conscious perception. Consciousness is what you are aware of. Your subconscious is all your automatic knowledge, like breathing or walking. You don't have to think about it, and you aren't aware of it. Somehow Ms. Dottie hacked their subconscious minds using subliminal audio. Subliminal audio is sound played at a level you are unable to hear consciously—but that your subconscious mind can perceive."

A'Lo's eyes glazed over. "So she tranced her competition."

BREAKING NEWS
BANNED FOR CHEATING

DESCENDANT OF MUSIC ROYALY AND AMERICAN IDOL RUNNER UP, MILENA DAVIS HAS BEEN BANNED FOR CHEATING.

"I firmly deny any accusations that I had anything to do with the unfortunate events that hurt my competitors."

I scrolled down further and found a picture of Ms. Dottie walking out of the studio after the producers canceled the season finale. The photo caption read, "'American Idol runner up, Milena Davis Banned for Cheating.' She told reporters, 'I firmly deny any accusations that I had anything to do with the unfortunate events that hurt my competitors. I plan to be back on the stage very soon. Ms. Dottie D. will NOT be silenced!'"

"Alright, let's grab Merlin and get out of here before Mrs. Anthony comes back with Principal Williams," Josephine said.

Merlin yelled, "Stand me up for an interview? I'll put that reporter in a body bag!"

A'Lo looked at Merlin then back to me, "You deal with him. I will thump him on the back of his long neck if I have to deal with him. NO CAP!"

I grabbed Merlin by the arm and rushed out the library doors. "We need more help," I said to A'Lo.

"Bet! Let's go get Roly. She's known that maniacal music teacher longer than we have."

"What about my interview?" called Merlin as we dragged him out of the library.

The word hypnosis is derived from the Greek word "hupnos," which means to sleep. OH, sorry, you guys. I think I was going too deep there. Merlin says that me being a genius makes me long-winded. So let's get to the point. Hypnosis is when a person is placed in a trance. Usually, the hypnotized person is put to sleep and then told how they will act when they wake up. Have you ever seen a movie or a show when a person would swing a clock in front of someone's eyes or make them watch a clock and say, "you are getting very sleepy?" That's probably the fake kind like in the last book where Madam Fifi fake-hypnotized Global.

But, scientists at Harvard did record changes in the brain of 57 people who were under hypnosis. They showed that "Two areas of the brain that are responsible for processing and controlling what's going on in your body show greater activity during hypnosis. Likewise, the area of your brain that's responsible for your actions and the area that is aware of those actions appear to be disconnected during hypnosis." https://www.healthline.com/health/is-hypnosis-real#effects-on-brain

Do some research yourself and see what you think!

CHAPTER 11

Where Merlin Loses it and Roly Comes Undone

As we walked down the 5th-grade hallway, Merlin turned his attention away from his imaginary fame and back to his love life. He started singing at the top of his lungs. "My baby girl, my baby girl! Where is my love? My baby girl?" Over and over again, he belted out those same ridiculous lines.

I stopped and grabbed Merlin by the front of his backpack straps. "MERLIN!" I yelled. "You need to get a hold of yourself. You are acting crazy! You like asteroids and planets, NOT SINGING!"

Merlin could not be deterred, "Oh Roly . . . My dear Roly," he crooned. "You will be my girl one day, and we will sing sweet tunes into the sunset." A'Lo fell out laughing and pointed his mom's disconnected cell phone at Merlin to record him on video.

"Delete it, or I'll turn you in for ID theft," I threatened. I shook Merlin one more time.

"Josephine! Take me to Roly so that I may sing to her like a beautiful songbird and win over her heart." Merlin begged.

"Come on, Big Merlin. I will take you right to her." A'Lo shook from laughing so hard.

"We have got to figure out how to break this trance before my brother humiliates himself for life."

I walked ahead of them because I could not stand to see my big brother this way. He was hopeless in this state. I knocked on the door of room 107 of art class with Mr. J. Like the painter, his real name was Jacob Lawrence, but he let the students call him Mr. J.

"Hi, Mr. J. May Roly be excused? We need to work out a few kinks in the music set for our competition this weekend."

"Josephine Montgomery. What an honor to see you! Your poem at the mayor's re-election ceremony was excellent," he said smiling. "Of course, Roly can come with you. She has already finished her sketches." Roly was already gathering her things.

The moment Mr. J closed the door and Roly walked with us down the hall, Merlin began declaring his undying love for her.

"Roly,
I know you barely know me,
But you make me smile like a bunny,
And I know you think that's funny,
But I really like bunnies."

Roly blushed. "Man, this is rich!" A'Lo called out. "Merlin has really lost all the stars in that galaxy-sized head of his."

Roly ignored A'Lo. She was still blushing when she turned to me. "So, you're Merlin's younger sister?"

"My name is Josephine," I said, shaking her hand. "And, my brother is not usually quite so . . . over the top?"

Roly giggled. "So, what's up? Does Ms. Dottie want us to run through the songs for the competition?"

Clearly, Roly was not aware of the situation at hand. "Not exactly," I said.

"Not exactly?" yelled A'Lo, pointing at Merlin. He had stopped reciting poetry and was now doing what looked like the cupid shuffle in the hallway while singing

Roly's name. "Do you not see the crazy going on here?"

Roly glanced at Merlin. "I have noticed Merlin acting a little weird, but don't all boys act weird sometimes?"

I had to agree that was true, but this behavior was out in left field and over the fence. "True," I replied, "But something more is happening. We believe Ms. Dottie has hypnotized the entire competition choir to make them sing better."

Roly tilted her head just a bit. "Oh, really?" she said as if she was just now understanding. "Let's talk about this in here," she said as she ushered us into the custodial closet.

"In the closet? What the…?" A'Lo switched on the light. There were mops and buckets crowded around us.

When my eyes adjusted, I thought Roly looked different. She reminded me of the stray cat that hung around my Dad's back patio right before it pounces on a lizard.

"So, bet. What do you think about Ms. Dottie going all…" before A'Lo could finish his thought, Roly went straight Yasuke on us. Yasuke, in some cultures, references a black ninja or an Afro Samurai.

As if she had superhuman strength, Roly grabbed one of the mops and ripped a handful of strings loose. A'Lo screamed for his life and tried to run. But before he could take a second step, she had his hands behind his back, wrapping them with mop strings!

Merlin yelled, "SWEEP THE LEGS!"

Before I could blink, Roly parkoured it up the closet wall and wrapped her legs around my neck! One minute we were talking, and the next, A'Lo and I were subdued on the floor!

"Merlin, don't just stand there!" I yelled at my love-dope brother.

He fell to his knees and offered his wrists to Roly, "Take me, my love!"

"Bruh, that is pathetic," A'Lo said, like he didn't just scream his head off.

Once she had us all restrained, Roly said, "I moved to this school to work with Ms. Dottie and to win a choir competition. I don't know what you all are talking about, but we are on track to winning, and I won't let anyone get in my way."

Merlin called out, "Finish them!"

"E'rbody's lost it up in this school!" A'Lo raised his tied hands in front of his face as Roly crouched down like a cobra ready to strike.

The situation looked dire, which means hopeless, but my mom taught me the power of positive thinking and faith. Mama says those two things can turn almost any situation around. I had nothing to lose, so I offered up Harriett Tubman's "Unconditional Affirmation." It's a prayer she used as she engineered escape plans for slaves on the Underground Railroad.

So I closed my eyes and said, *"I'm going to hold steady on You, an' You've got to see me through."*

Roly let out a small screech. I opened my eyes to see her looking at the three of us tied up on the floor, totally confused. Merlin was blinking his eyes like he had something in them. "What in the world?"

Roly whimpered, "Oh Josephine, A'Lo. What have I done?" Roly reached down and untied us.

I stood up with a smile on my face and hugged her. A'Lo backed up against the wall, still wary, which means nervous. "It's ok, Roly. I think you were under a trance," I said, giving her one last squeeze.

We all sat down on the floor of the custodial supply closet. Roly broke the silence first, "I can't believe this has happened. The last thing I remember clearly is me begging my mom to transfer me to another school after winter break."

"You mean, you didn't want to come here?" I asked.

Roly shook her head "no." She looked at the floor. "I loved my old school. I had lots of friends there. I've known Ms. Dottie almost all my life. At one of my singing lessons, I recall that she told me that the new school she was teaching at had a great program, and she wanted me to come. I told her no. She didn't seem upset and just started playing my solo on the piano," Roly said.

"That must have been it!' I had a revelation. "The piano! Ms. Dottie must have hypnotized you with trance music and convinced you to get your parents to transfer you." A revelation is when you understand an idea, and it comes into your mind very quickly.

Merlin stood up beside Roly and started to open the door. "I told y'all Ms. Dottie was up to something, but would y'all believe Big Monty? Noooooo!" A'Lo followed behind him.

"Big Monty? More like big Love Doofus! You should have heard your hypnotized self singing love songs to Roly and acting all loopy. HAHAHAHA!" A'Lo followed Merlin out of the closet, "'Finish him!' HAHAHAHA."

Merlin looked like he wanted to crawl into the floor. "Be quiet, Bad Breath," Merlin said. "There's a lot of crazy going on just like I thought, and if we don't act fast, Ms. Dottie may get exactly what she wants."

Roly knew some serious knots to tie up three people faster than you can say #goals. But my Dad says the most important knot you can know how to tie is a tie. A necktie. You won't look sharp in your job or college interview if you don't know how to tie a necktie. So go get one out of your dad or uncle's closet. Then, watch this video and send a picture of yourself looking ready to conquer the world to me on the @mattmaxxbooks Insta page. Or, if your parents are old school, they can look me up on Facebook!

https://www.youtube.com/watch?v=WfOiSxLZEfk

CHAPTER 12

A Mortified Merlin and One Radical Rapper

Man, I told y'all I wasn't trippin' about Ms. Dottie. What an absolute mess! Merlin here. I can't believe that I was lost in a trance for an entire day. I claim absolutely no responsibility for my behavior, and I'd appreciate it if we could just forget the whole embarrassing thing. Now that I am back, we have a lot of work to do. Roly and I snapped out of our trance, but we still have an entire class of students to dehypnotize before we all get in trouble for cheating and ruin our chances at going to college.

The day before the choir competition, we had one more rehearsal left. Josephine convinced our Dad to lend her a few packs of earplugs that he keeps in his lab for certain explosive experiments. Last week he burned his eyebrows off trying to concoct a chemical reaction to put the hair back on the butt of a baboon!

"Here is a pair of earplugs for each of you. They are meant to be incognito." Josephine told us, handing each of us a small biodegradable package with two little tan buds in them. By the way, incognito means concealed or hard to see. She continued, "Be sure to keep these in your ears while Ms. Dottie plays her keyboard, or you'll be tranced again, and we don't know how to reverse it."

A'Lo, Josephine, and Roly followed behind me into the classroom with their ears plugged. Josephine went to the back of the class to watch Ms. Dottie for clues on how to reverse this trance, and Roly and I went to the first row. The moment A'Lo linked up with Mabel, he was already back in full joke mode.

"Aye, Mabel, who am I?" A'Lo said, getting down on one knee like he was proposing. "Oh Roly, I love you!! MUA MUA!" he called out in a squeaky high-pitched voice. I wanted to DIE of embarrassment. But, before I could say anything to A'Lo, Ms. Dottie took her place at the front of the class.

"Everyone stand! Tomorrow is our competition, and this is our last practice. I want it to be perfect!" Ms. Dottie smiled at me. Josephine said we had to be sure to act like we were still hypnotized, but I didn't know how I was going to fake my solo.

Ms. Dottie began the first song, and my palms started sweating as my part grew closer. At the very moment, Ms. Dottie pointed her baton at me, I realized, being in a trance couldn't have affected my actual vocal cords. I took a deep breath from my diaphragm and let it rip. Ms. Dottie smiled, and I could tell I'd hit the notes I was supposed to. After the first song and Global's performance on the bassoon, Ms. Dottie called Josephine to the front of the room to recite her spoken word.

Roly whispered, "Merlin, we have to figure something out. The competition is in less than 24 hours." We were at a stalemate. A stalemate is a chess term meaning being stuck.

After Josephine's performance, we began our final song. I guess I was distracted and let my old, weak singing voice take the lead. I attempted to sing out, hoping that maybe I really did have a voice like Bruno Mars. From the look that Ms. Dottie gave me, I must have sounded like I was from Mars. Ms. Dottie started inching her way towards me, looking sus as heck. I began to panic. If Ms. Dottie figured out we weren't in her trance, we were finished.

Out of nowhere, A'Lo starts rapping. He pointed at me!

Check it! Check it!
Yo Miss Dottie, this song's a little shoddy,
won't you give me a chance
and give me a little spotty
because this dude right here's voice
  sounds like potty!

"Antavius LaRoyce Jenkins!" Ms. Dottie said. A'Lo *hates* to be called by his first name. A'Lo was HOT. He stepped out of his row to the front of the class. "Yo teach! I challenge you in a battle of rhymes!"

"A rap battle?" Ms. Dottie replied. "You are out of line. Go back to your seat!"

A'Lo had made his way to the front of the classroom. "Oh, I see, teach! You are scared when you can't *control* the outcome,' A'Lo said, flashing his metal fillings.

Ms. Dottie's eyes widened. She knew that A'Lo had figured out what she had done to the class. She returned a smile to A'Lo, vampire canines showing. "Alright, Antavius. Challenge accepted."

Ms. Dottie rolled up her sleeves.

> *A'Lo, is that your name?*
> *Sounds kind of sad, like your name is*
>   *a game.*
> *But I'm not a game, so you need a shift*
> *Passing my class ain't a thing but a gift.*

"OOOOOOOOOOH," the whole class said in unison. A'Lo's cheeks flushed, but he straightened his shoulders and went back in.

> *Ha Ha, very funny, Ms. Dottie's your name?*
> *I would not have guessed because they said you had fame.*
> *But that can't be true 'cause your rhyming is lame,*
> *which is no surprise because your skills are a shame.*

"BARSSSS!" Mabel yelled out.

The whole class cheered. A'Lo had really done it. The niece of a music genius was being shamed by a fifth-grade kid with a D average. My mom always said there were many different types of intelligence that school didn't measure, and A'Lo was solid proof. The dude was DEFINITELY smart.

As the class cheered, A'Lo bowed multiple times. Then, all of a sudden, his earplugs fell out and bounced on the floor. Ms. Dottie's eyes flashed as she understood how A'Lo avoided her trance. She flew to her keyboard and thundered out a trance chord. BLAM!

A'Lo stopped bowing immediately and stood straight as an arrow. "A'Lo, that will be enough. Please go back to your seat," Ms. Dottie said calmly. A'Lo was good and truly tranced. What were we going to do now?

CHAPTER 13

No Good Plans for One Hypnotized Class

On the day of the competition, Josephine and I tried to tell our mom we were sick. Josephine thought if we couldn't participate in cheating, we couldn't be held accountable for it. Then she could still go to whatever genius college she wanted to attend. We even held our foreheads in front of the toaster oven to make it feel like we had a fever, but mom whipped out her thermometer gun and told us we were just nervous.

I didn't feel right about that plan anyway. My best friend Global would be in trouble if the class got caught cheating in a school competition, even though he is a mean bassoon player without a trance. Then there was Roly, who really could sing. And even A'Lo had tried to stick his neck out to save us. One more infraction and that dude would spend eternity in Washington Carver Elementary. Ms. Dottie was risking all of our futures for a shortcut to success.

The entire bus ride to the competition, the class sat perfectly quiet. Even Mabel and A'Lo sat in their seats like perfect little choir soldiers. Josephine, Roly, and I all sat at the back of the bus. Roly was in a seat alone across the aisle. I whispered, "Man, what are we gonna do? This is jacked up."

Josephine's forehead was crinkled up, which meant her giant brain was churning. I still couldn't look Roly straight in the face after my performance this week. Talk about AWKWARD. Josephine was reciting her spoken word poem under her breath throughout the ride.

Backstage at the competition, the class huddled together. We all dressed in our competition attire, "penguin suits" of black pants or skirts and white shirts. In addition, all the students sported a patch with GWC on it in our school colors on our sleeves. Josephine flexed clothes out of her own closet, and hers was the only 'fit set off by polka dots. "Girl, you look fye!" A'Lo told her.

It was our turn to take the stage. Roly spoke up after not having said anything all morning. "Y'all, we really need to figure something out. Josephine, I wish you knew how you got Big Monty and me out of our trance in that broom closet." I smiled. It was the first time she said my name since A'Lo embarrassed us in front of the entire class.

"THAT'S IT," Josephine yelled out. One of the backstage crew members hushed her. Josephine whispered, "I got this, y'all. Don't worry." She threw back her shoulders and led the class on stage like it was totally normal for a second-grade kid to be in charge of a bunch of older students.

How to Make a Solar Oven: Cooking S'mores

While I was in a trance, I had these weird thoughts. One of them was kind of cool, though. A fun activity to play with your friend, with adult supervision, is to create a solar oven for smores. I may or may not have been thinking of ways to hang out with Roly and show her how cool science can be.

Materials:

- A small rectangular box, like an individual pizza box
- Craft scissors (Be sure to have an adult help you with those)

- Sharpies to decorate
- Black construction paper
- Aluminum foil
- Plastic sheet
- Glue
- Marshmallows, graham crackers, and a chocolate bar

Directions

This project should be done under the supervision of an adult and placed in direct sunlight.

1. Cut out a square in the top lid of the box to make the "oven door" flap.
2. Glue the black construction paper to the bottom of the box.
3. Glue the aluminum foil to the inside of the oven door.
4. Tape the plastic over the opening of the door to allow the box to heat up but keep the heat trapped inside the box.
5. Add a graham cracker, marshmallow, and chocolate inside the oven.

6. Place your oven outside in the sun. Use a stick or pencil to keep the oven door open to allow the sunlight to hit the plastic and to reveal the aluminum.

The smores should be cooked after being in the sun for about 90 minutes. While you wait, maybe go play a game with your friends.

CHAPTER 14

Last Ditch Efforts and All Tapped Out

Even if Josephine had an idea, the class was still hypnotized. We couldn't get caught cheating before Josephine executed her plan. In other words, we had to perform so poorly that no judge would ever accuse us of cheating.

As we filed out past the snack table, I grabbed a handful of popcorn faster than a lightning strike and shoved it in my pocket. Then, while Global set up the music stand for his bassoon, I dropped several kernels of popcorn into his instrument and took my place next to Roly.

The curtains opened. Ms. Dottie signaled the music booth, and our music for the first set began. During the first song, I sang out as loud as I could in my normal voice. Roly found it hard not to giggle. Ms. Dottie whipped her head in my direction and flashed her canine teeth. It was on like Donkey Kong. That maniacal music teacher knew we had her number.

Just then, Global started having trouble with his bassoon. Ms. Dottie's cut her eyes at him. Global took a deep breath and blew. A high screech came out of the bassoon and RAT TAT TAT TAT! Popcorn kernels started spraying out toward the judges' panel like open fire on GTA. One hit a judge square in the forehead, and she crawled under the table!

Ms. Dottie turned a deep shade of purple. The audience didn't know what to do. I noticed my parents in the third row. They got along well enough even though they split up years ago. My Dad was still wearing his work lab coat with goggles pushed up onto his forehead. My mom sat holding her extra-large-lensed camera between him and my Grandma P., but she wasn't taking any pictures. Global's mom looked mortified.

Josephine stepped to the front of the stage. Ms. Dottie carried the microphone to her keyboard. She announced, "We are honored to have Josephine Montgomery recite her award-winning poem "Memphis

Bred, Memphis Fed" today." Then, she hit a strong trance chord on the keyboard. BLAM! We had our earplugs ready. The rest of the class hit a perfectly harmonized background. Hmmm!

Josephine turned and gave us a thumbs up.

"I have been told
From young and old
That music feeds the soul
Much like a hot, buttered roll
Memphis born and Memphis bred
Music is the fuel that keeps us fed
Jackie Brenston sounded great
Made people croon with "Rocket 88"
And Sister Rosetta Tharpe
She added her heart
Music is the food of the soul
It's the perfect remedy for sadness for
*   those young and old*
So if you are watching anything I do
I'm going to hold steady on You, an'
***   You've got to see me through.'"***

Josephine had changed the last line of her poem to that Harriet Tubman prayer our mom always said! The whole class jerked awake and looked around like they didn't know where they were.

Roly whispered, "Your sister really is a genius. She figured out the words to break the curse!" Josephine placed the prayer she had mumbled that had knocked the sense back into me and Roly at the end of her poem, and the trance was broken.

"NOOOOOO!" Ms. Dottie shrieked. Josephine followed her last line with a curtsey and a smile. The entire audience stood up and broke into a mass applause. Ms. Dottie stood in front of us like a zombie. She had no choice but to continue conducting a choir full of un-tranced kids.

The first song after Josephine's performance went pretty well. After that, I decided to save our class any further embarrassment and gave the best lip-sync performance of my life. But the final song of our music set exceeded any of our expectations.

"Yo Merlin, switch spots with me," A'Lo whispered. I happily gave up my front row spot to A'Lo and took my original place on the 2nd row. A'Lo slowly moved in beside Roly. Ms. Dottie threw her hands up in despair at our rotation, and the final song began.

The final song set included a solo on the bassoon by Global, whose instrument was thankfully back to normal, and Roly as a soloist. Global opened with a set of tenor notes. Then, Roly came in with the sweetest, clearest notes you've ever heard. The auditorium grew silent.

LAST DITCH EFFORTS AND ALL TAPPED OUT

As Roly held a high D note, out of nowhere, here comes A'Lo with a drum beat. Rat, ta, tat, ta, tat rang out from the bottom of his shiny black shoes. That little joker tap danced out in front of the choir like Mr. Bo-freaking-Jangles himself! A'Lo slid, he turned, he jumped, and he tapped his too-small heart out while Global kept the music. Then he tapped his way over to Roly and pointed at her with guns. "Take it away!' And he tapped back into place beside her.

The audience roared in excitement. Global stood up and wiggled his hips around like he was Miles Davis on the Trumpet. Roly hit a high note and the rest of us joined in with everything we had.

Ms. Dottie started to regain her composure. Her conducting grew more and more enthusiastic as we picked up steam. I saw my Dad dancing so hard his goggles fell down to his neck. Everyone was clapping, dancing, stomping, and yelling out, "WCE! WCE! WCE!" for Washington Carver Elementary.

As we held our final note, A'Lo tapped his way over to Ms. Dottie and handed her a rose. She burst into tears, and we all took a bow.

CHAPTER 15

Real Wins and True Lessons Learned

"WOW! What a closing act!" Roly called out once we were backstage. The entire choir was all hyped up. A'Lo's crew was circling him, giving him knuckles. Ms. Dottie sat in a chair near the changing rooms in complete shock.

I walked up to Global, who was cleaning his bassoon. "Great job, man," I said. "I never would have thought you could pull off cool on that thing. You were fye out there."

Global smiled and said, "Never underestimate the nerds." I patted Global on the back and walked over to my sister, who was making her way toward Ms. Dottie.

"Hey, little sister! Hold up!" I called out. Josephine turned around, smiling from ear to ear. "Great job figuring out how to break the trance. I knew I could trust you with this mess." She reached out to give me a big hug, and this time, I let her.

Roly ran up to us. "Great job, Jo. Now let's go deal with Ms. Dottie."

Ms. Dottie ducked her head, ashamed as we approached. She said, "Such an amazing performance. I could not have asked for a better choir to work with,"

"Ms. Dottie, I am OVER the adults at Washington Carver acting cuckoo for Coco Puffs! What in the world possessed you to risk all our futures and CHEAT?" asked Josephine, hands on hips. She was so salty could see steam rising out of her puffballs!

"I am not surprised that you all figured it out. Josephine is not the only genius around," replied Ms. Dottie, looking at me. I blushed and looked away. "I am so sorry. The pressure of coming from a musical genius family just got to me. After I was banned from performing at American Idol, my life was ruined. All I ever knew was that I was supposed to be a musical success, and it seemed like all of that had crumbled beneath me."

Roly walked closer and sat beside Ms. Dottie. "But why did you drag me into this, Ms. Dottie?"

Ms. Dottie replied, "Roly, I am so sorry. I thought if I could win, you could get the attention you deserve for your talent. Of course, it was selfish, but that's how I justified it to myself. I was so desperate for success that I didn't even think about how I took you away from all of your friends."

Roly grabbed Ms. Dottie by the hand then looked up at Josephine and me. "I forgive you. Plus, I've made a ton of new friends."

"All I want to know is if you are done with your trance days," said Josephine. She was not so quick to forgive this teacher for almost blowing her chances at an Ivy League college in the second grade.

Ms. Dottie smiled and stood up. "I'm ready to get what I earn honestly," she said. "It's time for the awards ceremony." We followed her to our designated seats in the audience. I zoned out during most of the ceremony, but what I do remember was this. "Second Place in this year's Elementary School State Choir Competition goes to . . ."

That's right! We placed second. For some, that may feel like losing, but this was a true victory and an honest win after all the cracked stuff we went through.

After the ceremony, Josephine and I walked over to meet our folks. I saw A'Lo slide up to Roly. Their duet was off the chain. I was sure she would want to hang out with him since she knows that I actually can't sing. My mom grabbed both Josephine and me in for a hug, "Come on, mom! I got somewhat of a reputation to uphold," I said, trying to break loose.

When I finally escaped from my mom's death grip, I heard a giggle coming from behind me. I turned around and saw Roly standing behind our family, smiling. "Oh, hey Roly. I thought you had left," I said.

"Not yet, my folks are pulling the car around. But, I wanted to tell you that if you ever need singing lessons, I am free on Tuesdays," she said.

Josephine mumbled a soft, "oooooo," and my parents fell out giggling. I turned and gave them all a death stare.

"Oh, cool! That would be fun. I sure need the help." Roly reached over and gave me a quick hug. "See you Tuesday, Big Monty!" She said and ran out of the auditorium.

Josephine grabbed my hand and pulled me toward the exit, where white flakes were floating toward the ground. All our classmates were running around trying to catch snowflakes on their tongues and shrieking," It's snowing!"

"Come on, Romeo," Josephine said. "It's time to go home and make some sleds!"

Thanks for reading! We've had a nutty year at Washington Carver. Think we can make it until summer break without any more teachers crossing over to the dark side? You'll have to check in to www.mattmaxxbooks or follow us on IG or Facebook to find out! Meanwhile, here's one last project to keep you busy.

Peace,
Matt Maxx

Rainstick

Here's What You Will Need:

- Adult Supervision
- Empty Paper Towel Holder
- Craft Nails

- Funnel
- Hammer
- Clear Packing Tape
- Rice or Beans
- Wrapping Paper, Paint, or Duct Tape (optional for decorations)

Instructions:

1. Tape off the bottom of the paper towel tube with clear packing tape.
2. Place the first nail toward the end of the tube and hammer it in.
3. Rotate tube a ¼ of a turn, and place nail ½" – 1" below the top nail.
4. Continue this process all the way down the stick.
5. Pour rice and beans (your "rain") through a funnel into your tube.
6. Tape off open end.
7. Optional: Decorate rain stick with paper, paint or tape.

Made in the USA
Monee, IL
10 February 2023